Colson

The Adventures of Colson Matthews, Volume 1

Christopher Brueler

Published by Christopher Brueler, 2021.

This is a work of fiction. Similarities to real people, places, or events are entirely coincidental.

COLSON

First edition. November 7, 2021.

ISBN: 979-8201016494

Written by Christopher Brueler.

INTRODUCTION

This story goes on through the days of January 19th to January 23rd, in the year 2015. This whole story takes place in New York and occurs in the fictional town of Grainsbourg. This story focuses on Colson Matthews, an eighteen year old male who has recently discovered his best friend, Maxine Taylor, has gone missing. As stupid as it may sound, he wants to solve this case to find out where she may have gone, but not without someone tagging along, Megan Pryler. They'll try their best to find out what happened, together.

Chapter One: News

I'd be on a couch, drinking a cold glass of water. The TV was currently on a sports channel, specifically football. I'd turn off the lamp right next to me, as it was nighttime that this had happened.

I yawned, I was pretty tired, but that's when I had gotten a text. It was from my bestie, Maxine. It said this:

"Hey, I'll be going soon, bye."

I was super confused as to what she meant. Maybe she was hanging out with her girl friends? Probably, she was the type who partied a lot. I texted back:

"Alright, stay safe Max."

I then decided to put my phone away, after about fifteen minutes though, there was no text back from her. She was probably just partying.

I was about to sleep, but I fought the urge, and man am I glad that I did. If I had gone to sleep, I would have missed some very important news. I decided to turn the channel over to display the news, not even hours after she had texted me, she had gone missing.

"..Maxine? What happened to you? No no, this can't be real right? How could she? No, not her-" I said with disbelief in my voice.

I leaned forwards, the picture shown right next to the reporter had been one of her most recent. I know because she liked to send her selfies to people, like a lot.

It was one of her things I guess. Anyways, after learning of that news, I turned off the television relatively quickly. I went over to my laptop in my room and opened up my phone, I clicked on the picture and downloaded it. Man I sure am glad that she had sent that photo to me. She probably sent it to other people too though, since she had a selfie habit.

"Alright, missing person posters, right...." I got to work as soon as I got done speaking.

I sent the photo over to my computer, opened an app and started making some, just a few. After that was done, I printed them out and they were ready to go. Now, I need to sleep.

"This whole thing starts tomorrow.."

I lay my head on a pillow, and go to sleep. It'd probably be hard, knowing that she was still missing, but I'm not the world's greatest detective.

I still needed to get to the bottom of this.

Chapter Two: Beginning

I wake up with sweat all over my face, I take a heavy breath and get up. Having a nightmare about finding her dead wasn't exactly something I was looking forward to. I shake my head and quickly find some clothes to take a shower with, maybe that will help me with all the thoughts swirling around in my head right now. I doubt it.

"No way, she's not dead, she can't be. I'll find her and bring her back alive." I had a look of determination, I was going to solve it.

After saying that a few more times, I splash some water on my face. I don't know how'd that help, but I did it. Taking a shower helped.... none. I sigh and put my clothes on, I then take my bag and place the posters from yesterday in them. I'd place them up at lunch, I take a deep breath before heading over to my school.

Skip fifteen boring minutes of walking and I'm here, barely on time as well. As you could imagine, the whole school was talking about the "kid who had gone missing". My friend who had been there for me for years, I hadn't done much to pay her back either, I needed to show that I cared for her. Plus, she was my frickin' bestie, how could I not go trying to find out where she went? Just in case you were wondering, I went to the College of Grainsbourg, yes that was the name, deal with it. I sighed heavily as I looked around the school.

None of these people cared as much as I did, no one did. They wouldn't go on a whole investigation looking for her now would they? I shook my head, I was just hurt. Knowing that she was missing and all, but maybe if I keep telling myself I'll find her alive. Enough thinking, the bell for the first class had rung. I get over there as quickly as I can.

On my way there, though. I accidentally bumped into this kid, I looked up and saw Michael Fransier. The guy was a nice kid, too bad he was so shy. He looked embarrassed. Michael wasn't a bad guy at all, super nice. He was a skinny asian boy, about five foot nine.

"Sorry, I bumped into you didn't I-" Michael would bow hesitantly, poor kid.

"You're fine man, don't worry about it." I would shrug it off, I didn't mind being bumped into, unless it was on purpose.

"You sure?" I could tell that he was fearful of me, it was sad to see really, he was bullied so much.

I nodded.

"Why wouldn't I be? Don't worry man, you're cool." I smiled and patted him on the shoulder

I genuinely felt bad for him, the kid deserved so much yet he got so little. I patted him on the back as I walked off towards my class.

"Say, want to hang sometime?" I guess I just wanted to ask, I was kind of bored so yeah, I wanted to hang out with someone.

"Yeah, uh, sure. Thank you." I saw that a small smile came onto his face, it made me feel glad.

I nodded, every time I'd see Michael I'd try to be kind. I saw him as a friend. It was time to get to my class now though, both of us went our separate ways. Me and Michael were slowly building up to best friends, I could feel it.

The classes were pretty much the same, boring. Nothing really happened, I saw Michael a few times and chatted with him though, it was nice, building up my friendship with him. You could say I trusted him a lot now. Fast forward to lunch. I didn't even bother to get one, I just went straight into the hallway because we're allowed to do that, for some reason. I had made sure to bring tape with me, fortunately. I took another heavy breath and started putting up the posters, when I was on my third one however, I heard footsteps behind me.

I quickly turned around, but the person was a fellow student. A female student, I look at her with a bit of curiosity. Had she followed me here? She however, ignored my look and went straight towards the posters.

"So, you're putting up posters? Are you looking for her by any chance?" She said with a smirk on her face, it was like she knew what I was up to.

She then gave a look of suspicion, I tried my best to come up with some sort of lie.

"Yeah uh, no, I was just uh-" I stuttered, nice job, idiot. You made it obvious.

She then cut me off.

"You are such a horrendous liar, don't worry, I won't let anyone know." The mystery girl would put a finger over her mouth, she was definitely a little weird.

She said the last part with a whisper. I was going to say something, but she interrupted me again.

***Her:** "That is, if you let me help you."*

I couldn't believe it, was she really doing this? Why would she want to help me? We barely knew each other. I stutter a bit before I manage to say something.

***Me:** "Why would you want to help me?"*

She answered my question, but not the way I had really hoped that she would.

***Her:** "I have my reasons, Megan, by the way. Nice to meet you, Colson."*

I was simply baffled by how she knew my name already, but I remember that she was in my third class with me. She must have heard my name during attendance. I awkwardly waved towards her as she walked off.

***Me:** "Nice to meet you? It's Colson, I guess we can start this whole thing later?"*

***Megan:** "I guess so, just give the address at the end of the day."*

***Me:** "Right, see ya then."*

Well, I guess I have a partner helping me now, after about two hours the school day was over. Somehow she knew exactly where I was, as I was walking out the front door she had stopped me. I had almost forgotten, I nodded and wrote the address of my house down, I gave her the piece of paper and we nodded at each other.

I then walk out of the building and start walking towards the direction of my house. Luckily it wasn't too far. About fifteen minutes later and I'm here, I grab my keys and unlock the door. I walk inside.

Me: *"Alright, it's been an okay day, maybe a snack will fix my mood?"*

I fix a turkey sandwich and put mayonnaise on it, I don't care what anyone says, it is good. Anyways, that didn't do anything to my mood, as expected. I was taking another bite into my sandwich, but I was interrupted by a knock on the door. She was here, I went over to the door and opened it for her.

Me: *"Welcome to my house, I spent some time cleaning up and everything. Make yourself comfortable."*

Megan: *"Sure."*

She looks over towards the kitchen and looks at me, did she want something? I lifted an eyebrow before her gaze shifted away from me. She sat down by the table.

Me: *"You hungry? I could fix something up if you want."*

Megan: *"If you want, but you know that's not what I'm here for."*

Me: *"Yeah, I know."*

I walked over to the kitchen and fixed her a turkey sandwich really quickly. I placed it in front of her and she nodded. I saw a slight smile escape from her lips before I sat down myself. We both take a bite.

Megan: *"So, how do you plan to start this whole thing?"*

Me: *"I honestly don't know, as crazy as it sounds, she may be in some hospital or something. We could try those first."*

Megan gives me a look of confusion.

Megan: *"Now why would she be in a hospital?"*

I shrug.

Me: *"I don't know, maybe she got hurt while she was out and someone found her?"*

Megan: "Maybe, but I doubt this will work, we should try asking family first. You got any info on them?"

I nod, I had been over her house a few times since she and I did have quite the relationship.

Me: "Yeah, I'll see if I can find anything that'll take us there."

Megan: "Alright, make it quick. I can't stay for long, I need to go back."

Me: "Got it, hey, how'd you get here by the way?"

She gave me another look of confusion.

Megan: "My car? Hello?"

Me: "Right, totally knew that you had a car."

She chuckled lightly, I ignored her and went into my room. If I didn't keep anything here, it was probably on my phone. I start by looking underneath my bed, nope. Maybe in the drawers somewhere? Just clothes, nevermind.

Megan: "Hey, have you found any leads yet?"

Me: "Nope, can you help me real quick?"

Megan: "Of course, I'll see what I can do."

Megan would join me in looking for anything that can help us find her parents. I get out my phone and open it with the passcode. While she was looking there, I'd scroll through my message history with Max. These are said messages I looked at:

January 15th, 2015 at 4:59 PM: "Hey Maxine! How has your day been so far?"

January 15th, 2015 at 5:00 PM: "It's actually been alright, I'm fine though, don't worry!"

January 15th, 2015 at 5:01 PM: "You sure? I don't want you feeling sad you know?"

January 15th, 2015 at 5:01 PM: "I'm sure Col! Everything's alright! Say, you want to come over sometime?"

January 15th, 2015 at 5:02 PM: "Sure, I'm down to come over!"

January 15th, 2015 at 7:09 PM: "Alright, I'll let you know the address tomorrow!"

January 16th, 2015 at 5:20 PM: "Colson! Show up at the blue house on Red Viking Rd. and I'll meet you there!"

January 16th, 2015 at 5:30 PM: "Sorry for the late response, I'll be there shortly!"

That was it, although it wasn't an exact address it still worked. I had a little moment to celebrate before turning to Megan, who looked like she had searched the whole place.

Megan: *"Hey, sorry, I wasn't able to find anything, you?"*

Me: *"It's alright Megan, really. I found something. Let's go!"*

Megan: *"Alright, we'll take my car!"*

We both run outside, in a hurry to get into the car. After we were in, we started going fast.

Megan: *"So tell me, where are we going?"*

Me: *"The blue house on Red Viking Rd."*

Megan: *"Huh? That's it? What about the-*

She would laugh a bit, yeah, my friend wasn't really good with directions. Just thought I'd tell you that.

Me: *"Yeah, she wasn't really good with directions."*

Megan: *"Well, it's something we could use. As long as it's useful I'll take it. Blue house on Red Viking road here we come!"*

Me: *"Hey, uh, would you mind slowing down a bit? You're going a little too fast and it might get us pulled over."*

Megan: *"Oh yeah? My bad."*

Me: *"Yeah, thanks."*

After talking about pretty much nothing for five minutes, we arrive at Red Viking road. We both look out for a blue house.

Megan: *"You said a blue house right? I'm not really seeing any over here."*

Me: *"Keep looking, it's probably somewhere around here."*

Chapter Three: Clues

We were still driving, but eventually, after a few minutes we had found the house. I let out a sigh of relief, Maxine's family hadn't moved after all. Megan got out of the car and stretched before bringing her gaze over to the house.

Megan: "That's the house?"

Me: "Yeah, we're here."

She nods before motioning me to come with her, we both walked up towards the door and knocked. After about a minute, two people answered, by the looks of them they were Max's parents. I knew them, considering I had come here three days earlier.

The mother was Stacy, the father was Max. They both shook my hand before welcoming me inside.

Max: "Well, who's this you've brought with you young Colson?"

Stacy: "She's probably just a friend, Max."

He gave a good look at Megan, she quickly introduced herself to the both of them and smiled.

Megan: "Yeah, it's nice to meet you sir."

Max would nod and back away, he seemed sorry. He and Stacy invited us over to the table to eat with them.

Me: "Actually, I just ate so-"

Max: "Come on, a little food never hurt anybody!"

Megan: "Sir, I'd like some if you don't mind."

I sigh.

Me: "Alright, I'll eat some too."

Max: "Well alright, what do you two want?"

I looked towards Megan. Asking about their missing daughter didn't feel right, not at all. If we wanted to solve this case though, it was necessary. I take a deep breath before I look at the both of them.

Me: *"I'll feel horrible for asking this but, do any of you know where Maxine is?"*

They both shook their heads, maybe I could try asking them where she told them where she was going. That could get us somewhere. I took a bite of the spaghetti before I said anything.

Somehow though, Megan pretty much knew exactly what I was going to say, and we both said it at the same time.

Me & Megan: *"Where did she tell you she was headed?"*

They both looked at us and sighed, I could understand how they were feeling at this moment. I felt horrible for even bringing her up.

Max: *"Well she told us she was going to some sort of party with her girl friends."*

Stacy: *"She said she'd be back at eleven-fifty, but we haven't seen her for about twenty hours now.*

Max: *"She hasn't been answering her phone at all, we tried about fifty times calling her."*

They both take a moment to not say anything, after hearing that how could you not feel bad for them?

Me: *"I am.. horribly sorry this has happened to you, no one deserves to lose their child. I know how tough it is on you."*

Megan: *"Yeah, we needed to know if you knew any of her possible whereabouts so we could try and find her and return her to you safely."*

They couldn't believe what they had heard, I could tell since they both gave us a look of shock.

Max: *"You'd really do that? You're risking your lives-"*

Me & Megan: *"We know."*

Stacy: *"Maxine is so lucky to have people that care about her this much, are you sure? This is risky business."*

Megan: *"Ma'am, we're sure about this."*

Me: *"Yeah, she's my best friend, besides she's done so much for me. I think it's time I repay her."*

Megan: *"I tagged along because well, it seems she means a lot to Colson here."*

The two parents would look as if they were about to tear up, we still needed to ask something though. The name of the girls she said she was "partying" with.

Me: *"May we ask another question if you don't mind?"*

They both nod.

Me: *"By any chance do you know the name of the girls she said she was going to have fun with?"*

Stacy takes a step forward and nods.

Stacy: *"When I asked who, she said-"*

Me: *"I'm sorry ma'am, I just need to get some notebook paper and a pen so I can write this down, do you have that by any chance?"*

Stacy: *"Of course, check in Maxine's room."*

I nod and motion for Megan to follow me, I had been around this house a couple times before, so I knew it pretty well. Max's room would be three rooms down to the right. We enter and I start to search for some paper for both of us.

Megan: *"Tell me when you found something, I'll be right here by the doorstep."*

Me: *"Got it."*

Not even five minutes after she said that, I had found the paper. I gave one to her and kept one for myself. We went back out into the living room and into the kitchen, where the parents were waiting.

Me: *"Sorry for the wait, go on ahead please."*

Stacy: *"Right, these girls, she only told me one of them. Joanna Fritz, I'm not sure where she is but hopefully that helps."*

I wrote down her name first, and then gave the pen to Megan, who also wrote the name down. This could help, knowing her first and last name. We'd have to ask this individual a couple of questions once we got there.

Me: *"Joanna Fritz, right?"*

I lifted my eyebrow and placed the pen down on the paper.

Stacy: *"Yes, that's who it was, I remember it as clear as day."*

Me & Megan: *"Alright, thanks both of you. We appreciate it!"*

We both got out of our seats and prepared to leave, but the parents clearly wanted to say something else.

They walk over to the both of us and pat us on the head.

Stacy: *"Thank you for being so brave, I really hope you find our daughter. Be careful."*

Max: *"Thank you, both of you better stay safe. We appreciate you so much."*

Megan: *"Of course, I hope we find your daughter too, Mr. and Mrs. Taylor."*

Me: *"Alright, we must leave now, thanks for the food by the way."*

We all wave goodbye and part from one another, Megan drives back to my house and then goes back to her own. We must prepare ourselves for tomorrow.

Chapter Four: Gear Up

January 20th, 2015: *Yesterday was insane, super insane. I couldn't sleep at all, I was worried I'd have another nightmare or something. I sigh and get out of bed, finding some clothes and taking a quick shower.*

After the shower I'd walk to school, the usual. Again, it took about fifteen minutes to get there. Nothing really too interesting happened, then I realized I never got to finish hanging up the posters yesterday. Right, I needed to do that. The bell rang and I went to my first class of the day.

Yet again, fast forward to lunch and I'm in the hallway again, except this time I noticed something, some idiots had ripped the posters off. Jerks. I spent about the whole lunch period putting up those posters. I got about seven up before I was caught by the faculty.

Mrs. Rose: *"Hey, I find it sweet that you care about her so much, but could you please get some lunch? Here, I'll put them back up for you."*

Mrs. Rose was honestly one of the kindest teachers ever, note that I may have had a little crush on her. How could I not? She was really pretty, and really nice to everyone. She was honestly just amazing. She had a husband though, and was too old for me anyways. Aside from that, when I nodded at her I just suddenly knew that Megan was there.

Me: *"Right, thank you Mrs. Ro-"*

Megan: *"Come on loverboy, let's go. I need to talk to you."*

My facial expression suddenly went from calm to embarrassed. She really had a big mouth didn't she? I nodded towards Megan and walked past Mrs. Rose, embarrassed of myself. The teacher didn't even know where to begin, she didn't say a word. Thanks, Megan.

Me: *"Right, so what do you want to talk about Megan?"*

She could see that I was still blushing from what had happened from before not too long ago. She simply just laughed it off and patted me on the back.

Megan: *"Aw, did I embarrass you? Come on, she'll get over it!"*

Me: *"I guess so, but if you ever do that again I'll be sure to spill anything I know about you."*

Megan: *"Chill, she probably thinks I'm joking, everyone knows I like to joke a lot."*

Me: *"Hopefully so, so what is it you want to talk about?"*

Megan: *"So later today, we need to gear up."*

Me: *"What exactly do you mean by "gear up?"*

She wouldn't have time to tell me, the bell had rung already. We needed to get to our classes.

Megan: *"Alright, I'll see you later, partner."*

Me: *"Yeah, see you later Megan."*

As I was walking to my fifth class, I was shoved by someone I didn't really recognize, but when I looked up I knew who it was instantly. Of course it was the "toughest" guy at the school, Tye Andrews. Standing at six feet five with a slim, fit figure, green eyes, white hair and pale skin. He had seen me with Megan, which I assume he thought was my girlfriend.

Tye: *"Listen, you dating one of the smartest girls in school makes no sense. Back off, she's mine, buddy.*

I wasn't really intimidated at all, I just stared at him with a blank expression. It seemed to tick him off because next thing you know, I'm against a locker.

Tye: *"Stay away, you hear me?"*

Me: *"Yeah, sure dude."*

He smirked before letting me drop on my bum, which hurt a little, but I was fine. I brush off my clothes and gather all of my stuff again to get to class.

The bell for the final class rang, and I started walking over towards my house. As soon as I got outside however, Megan was there in her car, waiting for me. I really needed one of my own.

Megan: "Come on, we got some work to do."

Me: "Yeah, tons of it."

I get into the red station wagon and we drive off towards my house. Megan once again taps me on the shoulder to tell me something. What I didn't notice was that Tye was watching me drive off with her.

Megan: "Alright so first, you know that we can't tell anyone about this right? We have to do this in secret, only people we can tell are Maxine's parents, and we already told them."

Me: "Yeah, I know."

I nod to confirm that I had already known that.

Megan: "Cool, so that's why we need a disguise. You know, for our detective work and stuff."

Me: "Yeah, that makes sense. So where are we going?"

Megan: "First, we'll probably ask for some money-"

Me: "No it's fine, I have some at the house we can use, I've been saving up."

Megan: "Well that was convenient, alright, guess we'll make a pitstop at your house then."

She accelerates towards the destination of my house, what was it with her and going so fast on the road?

Me: "Hey uh, can you slow down please?"

Megan: "Oh, right, forgot you had a weak stomach."

Me: "No that wasn't it-"

Megan: "I know, just joking."

Me: "Wow, you'd be a great comedian then."

That comment got me a punch directed at my arm. I rubbed it and chuckled a bit, she got a good laugh out of it too.

We're here now, my house. We both get out of the car and I pull out my keys. Just as I was about to open my door though, I heard a yell not too far from here. I look over to see who it was, it was of course Tye, the school bully. How'd he even get here? Right, forgot he somehow had a car as well.

Tye: *"Hey kid, think you look tough in front of your girlfriend? I'll show you who's the toughest around here."*

I sigh, I ignore him and put the key in the lock anyway.

Megan: *"Who is that? How did he even get here?"*

Me: *"I don't know, but it's clear he's looking for a fight."*

Tye didn't like the fact that I ignored him, because he ran up from behind and grabbed me, proceeding to shove me onto the ground. Now that wasn't too bad of a hit, I recovered quite quickly.

Tye: *"You've got no choice, you'll have to fight your way out of this one, buddy."*

Me: *"So I conclude on the fact that you have been watching me, correct?"*

Tye simply growls and takes a swing towards my left, now I wasn't much of a fighter, but I was fast on my feet. I quickly move towards the right, where I then proceed to shove him. Now I wasn't too bad myself. Six foot one, slim figure, brown eyes and brown skin. I got hit by one of his punches, which connected with my nose.

The hit sent me back, that's for sure. Before I had time to recover though, I got hit by another one towards the chin. After that, I got a little ticked myself, I managed to tackle him to the ground. We started to twist and turn around before I managed to get him on his back, I then landed one good punch right on the eye before I got up and managed to rush into the house with Megan, who was still waiting by the doorstep by the way.

Megan: *"Jeez that was wild, you alright Colson?"*

I nod. A little blood was nothing to worry about.

Me: *"Yeah, I'll be fine, let's just find the money and get back to the car quickly."*

Megan: *"Right, got it."*

I opened my drawer and collected the money, I then got up and told Megan to follow me.

Me: *"I got the money, let's go. Tye should still be on the ground."*

I was wrong, Tye was long gone, probably embarrassed that he didn't really do anything to me. I shrug it off and let Megan open the door to the car before we drove off towards a store.

Me: "Which store are we going to?"

Megan: "You know, the one that sells clothes."

Me: "Very specific, I like it."

Megan: "Oh shut up."

After talking about pretty much nothing for five minutes, we arrived at the store. The lights were lit green as it flashed:

"WELCOME TO ALLEN'S GOODS! ENJOY YOUR SHOPPING!"

Me: "Alright, what will we find here?"

Megan: "What we need, now let's go."

I sighed and got out of the car, once we were in the store, Megan and I went up to the cashier. She asked me for money and I gave it to her, it was about $300 worth of cash, alright, that wasn't all I was saving up either. It was just enough to get us some clothes here.

I looked around to see tons of outfits, none didn't really look too detective-y, well, a black trench coat with a brown Homburg hat and black cowboy boots looked good. That's what I thought at least.

Detective (Colson): Black trench coat w/o buttons and a Homburg hat. (Black and brown) with black sweatpants.

Megan: "Hey, looking good Colson!"

Me: "You think? Yeah, thanks. Now it's time to find your disguise."

Megan: "Right, let's see here.."

Detective (Megan): Cotton light brown trench coat w/o buttons and dark sunglasses with her hair tied back in a ponytail and khaki pants

Me: "What are you going to do about your long hair?"

I really should have given a description of her appearance. She had long brown hair, pale skin, and black eyes. She simply tied her hair back as a response to my question.

Me: "If that somehow works-"

Megan: "It will, trust me, I'm a master of disguise."

I sighed heavily and rolled my eyes, we thanked the cashier on our way out and got back into the car before driving off towards my house. It was time to start this thing, for real.

Once we got there we knew it was time to get onto the case of my best friend, Maxine. We tried the laptop, but it didn't really work. All of the sites we tried using needed credit card info, and I didn't really trust that. I closed the laptop and started pacing around the room, Megan saw this and looked at me with great concern in her eyes.

Megan: "Hey, we didn't get this far to just quit. We need to keep trying."

Me: "This isn't for us Megan, we can't try and solve something we don't know how to solve."

Megan: "I'm sure we'll find something, now stop giving up and let's do this."

Me: "Alright, I'll try again, I need my friend back."

Megan: "Good, now come over here and let's keep looking."

I nodded and sat down beside her, we looked on site after site. Nothing, would this be the end? We had gone through at least twenty sites by now, still nothing. It was about five hours until we found something. It looked like a shady website, but when we clicked on the link, it led us to some sort of video. It showed a guy who looked to be in his early thirties sitting in front of a webcam. We stared at each other as we watched the video play.

Man: "Welcome to my site, now that you have clicked on it, you can't get out. You'll have to let me help you, Colson Matthews and Megan Pryler."

We backed away from the screen as we watched in pure terror, this guy knew our names? How was that even possible? He started laughing, probably at how scared we were. He continued to speak.

Man: "Don't worry, I don't plan on hurting you, I want to help you. I know how you two are playing detective and are trying to find someone."

Me & Megan: "But how?"

Man: "Your clothing makes it quite obvious, meet me at 45940 Xavier Street, I'll be waiting to give the address to you."

He left with a laugh of pure craziness, this guy was totally a nutjob. Me and Megan look at each other once more. What did we just get ourselves into? I sigh and pull down my hat.

Me: "You think we can trust him?"

Megan: "Definitely not, that's why we need something for self defense."

Me: "What do you mean?"

Megan: "Let's go."

She grabs onto my arm and pulls me out of my own house, next thing you know we're at a gun store that is just simply called

PISTOLS AND RIFLES

Me: "What exactly are we doing here, Megan?"

Megan: "What do you think? Come on."

We both go into the store, still in our detective disguises. I look around at all of the handguns, rifles, and all different types of guns we could buy here.

Me: "Are you sure this is a good idea?"

I whisper, she whispers back.

Megan: "Stop being a wuss, you're of age to buy a handgun."

Me: "Right."

A few minutes later, I have a Beretta 92, and Megan has a SIG Sauer P220. We were ready in case this was a trick of some sort.

Megan: "Better put that in one of your pockets, Colson."

Me: "Yeah, I know, you best put yours in there too."

Megan: "Mhm."

Chapter Five: Joanna

We were still driving towards the destination the man had told us to come to. Luckily for the both of us, I had a pretty good memory. I looked towards Megan, I already knew what she was going to say.

Me: "45940 Xavier Street is our exact location if you were wondering."

She gave me a look that showed that she was speechless and amazed.

Megan: "You totally knew what I was going to say? Wild, guess you learned from me."

Me: "Sure, I'll say that."

She chuckled as a response to my statement.

Megan: "Alright, hold on tight, we're going to go a little faster!"

She wasn't kidding either, we were going pretty fast down the road now. Well, at least she didn't drive like a maniac.

Me: "Let's see if this man is actually trustworthy or not."

Megan: "Yeah, if not, I'll be popping a cap in his temple."

Me: "You know, that sounds a lot less intimidating if you say it like that."

Megan: "As long as you get what I meant by that, I couldn't really care less."

I simply nodded as we sped off towards 45940 Xavier Street. We were about ten minutes away from it now.

Megan: "Best get yourself ready in case you need to kill someone."

Me: "Yeah, I get it."

I gulped, hopefully no killing would be done. We could only hope for the best now, neither of us wanted to use these guns.

Fast forward another ten minutes of nothing and we were at our destination. We both got out of the car and made sure our guns were out of sight. Luckily the pockets were quite huge on these trench coats.

Megan: *"Where is he? He said meet him here."*

Me: *"Get ready, I have a bad feeling about this."*

We started to look around the entire area, both of us heard nothing for a split second before we heard footsteps approaching. After those footsteps we were on alert.

Megan: *"Who's there? We can hear you!"*

Me: *"It might be him, but if not, then.."*

We both swiftly pulled out our handguns, ready to shoot if necessary. There was no need though, since it was just the man from the website. He came out with his hands up in the air.

Man: *"Hey, put the guns away, there's no need."*

Megan: *"How exactly do we know that?"*

Man: *"You'd be dead by now if this was a trick, calm down."*

I put my gun down first, and then Megan put hers down as well. We both kept looking around us to make sure no one was here.

Man: *"Alright, stay calm kids. I'll even give you my name, Trevor. Does that convince you?"*

We look at each other and sigh, we place our guns in our pockets as Trevor placed his hands down. He looked in his early thirties. He had a skinny figure, greasy, pulled back hair, brown eyes and skin the color of sand.

Trevor: *"There you go, now we can get to business."*

Me: *"First off, do we need to pay you anything?"*

Trevor: *"Aw come on, you're kids, consider this my kind deed to help you out like this."*

Megan: *"Why us? Why are you deciding to help us when there are other real detectives out there?"*

Trevor: *"Listen, I've worked with tons of detectives."*

Me: *"How are we supposed to believe that?"*

Trevor: *"Now is not the time for this, you want to find your friend don't you?"*

Me: *"Yeah, you're right. So what's the address?"*

Trevor: *"Follow me to my house, I'll show you how I do it to make this go by faster for you two. You're on a time limit here."*

Me & Megan: *"Time limit?"*

Trevor: *"Of course, police, fellow detectives. Stuff like that."*

Megan: *"I suppose that makes sense."*

Trevor: *"Exactly, now get in your red station wagon and let's go."*

Me and Megan both get into the red car as Trevor gets into his brown SUV, we drive off towards his house.

Megan: *"What if there are men at his house? We won't know what's in there until we get inside."*

Me: *"Yeah, our guns won't be able to help us with that one. Especially if they're armed too."*

Megan: *"Hey, we might have a chance, I can beat some up and you can use your fast reflexes to dodge and shoot."*

Me: *"I don't think that would work."*

Megan: *"You never know."*

Me: *"You think he's watching us right now?"*

Megan: *"Yeah no, he would have said something otherwise."*

Me: *"I guess he would have, well, let's see how his house looks."*

Megan: *"Hey Colson, I've been wanting to ask this question for a while now but I never really got the chance."*

Me: *"Oh yeah? What's up?"*

I take my glare off of the road and look at Megan to see what she wanted to say, she took a heavy breath before asking her question.

Megan: *"How come your parents don't stop you from doing this? Sorry if this is personal, but I was just curious."*

I shake my head to signify that it was fine, I had actually never told her about my parents.

Me: "They could care less about what I do now, it was nice growing up with them and all, but when I reached seventeen and was almost eighteen they just stopped caring all of a sudden, gave me some money, bought a house for me and sent me off."

Megan: "Holy... how long have you been living in that house of yours?"

Me: "About six months now, I haven't seen them in a decently long time."

Megan: "Jeez, I never knew. I'm sorry for asking, Colson."

Me: "It's alright, not like I care much or anything. What do you tell your parents whenever you go out to help me with this stuff?"

Megan: "I don't tell them, they're usually at work all the time anyways, so that's why I need to get home by at least ten."

Me: "I see, how are your parents?"

Megan: "They were laid back before, let me go to a friend's house whenever I wanted. That was until one day when one of the savages had tried to make out with me. Destroyed my trust completely. They started being super strict and I can see why, but I've met people like you that helped slowly rebuild said trust. I've tried to tell them so many times that I can actually trust them but they don't listen."

Me: "Sounds like they're just protecting you to me, nothing wrong with that."

Megan: "Yeah but, I want to have fun sometimes you know? You're a cool dude Colson."

She pats me on the back.

Me: "Thanks, Megan. You're pretty good yourself."

With that, we weren't too far from the house now. Trevor had made a couple lefts by the time we were done talking.

Me: "Well, we're almost there."

Megan: "Yeah, I need to get home in a couple hours though, so hopefully this is quick."

A couple of minutes later, we were finally at the house. We both had a little sigh of relief before we got out of

Megan's car. I took a quick look at the house, which actually didn't look bad at all. It looked as if it were a three story house and was painted yellow with a hint of white. It had lamps surrounding the outside and seemed as if it had a backyard.

__Me:__ "Jeez, Trevor looks as if he's living the life."

__Megan:__ "Indeed, that's a very nice house."

Trevor noticed us talking and motioned for us to follow him, once we were inside it looked like one of those houses from the mid-1900's. There were tons of chandeliers everywhere, accompanied by sofas, a TV, and wooden chairs. That was the living room though. Trevor had invited us into the kitchen.

__Trevor:__ "Take a seat, we'll talk at the dinner table."

His hands would point towards literally the only table in the kitchen, like we didn't notice. It was nice of him though, we sat down in the two chairs that faced the windows, Trevor sat right in front of us.

__Trevor:__ "Hold on, let me bring my computer down here."

He had gone upstairs before we could have said a single word, we decided to just wait. After a few minutes of hearing him yell, he came back down with the computer and cleared his throat before apologizing.

__Trevor:__ "I am deeply sorry, I was just looking for my computer."

Me and Megan looked at each other before nodding.

__Megan:__ "It's fine, but please make this quick, I need to go soon so-"

__Trevor:__ "Of course, almost forgot you kids were still in school."

He sighed before shaking his head, what was up with him?

__Trevor:__ "Alright, I'm wasting your time so I'll tell you how to do all of this later. Just go to 59830 Grace Boulevard and keep going until you see a white mansion, you'll find her there.

__Megan:__ "That's it? Well we'll take it. Again do we need to pay you or-"

__Trevor:__ "GO."

His tone shifted from that of calm to a more angered and menacing tone.

Megan quickly arose from her seat before telling me to get up. I was surprised at how fast his mood changed, I nodded and got up, we left without saying another word.

We got into the station wagon and drove off, it was time to pay Joanna a visit.

It was time to get to business, we had arrived at about nine-thirty. We nodded at each other and silently walked up towards the door. I told Megan to stay back, I would be the one who'd knock.

I knocked about five times before someone answered the door, it was a girl who looked to be about nineteen. She looked like she hadn't slept in ages, the girl looked at me with a deadpan stare.

Girl: *"Who are you two? Don't you realize how late it is?"*

Me: *"Yeah, we're just detectives. Are you Joanna Fritz by any chance?"*

She took a deep breath, as if I had annoyed her or something.

Joanna: *"That's me, what about it?"*

Chapter Six: Enemies

Me: *"We need to ask a few questions if you don't mind."*

    Megan: "Would you please let us inside so we can talk?"

Joanna: "Well, if you two actually are detectives I might as well."

She opens the door and moves out of the way, allowing us inside. We both nod towards her as a way of saying "Thank you."

Joanna: "Why don't you two sit on the couch in the living room? We can talk there."

Me: "Got it, thanks."

Megan: "Yeah, thanks."

The house was completely pitch black, that was until Joanna had turned on the kitchen light, which had helped us see a little bit. I took off my hat and placed it to the right of me as I took a seat. Megan would sit right next to me as we waited for Joanna.

Joanna: "Would you two like something to drink?"

Me: "That'd be great, but not right now."

Megan: "We're good, thanks though."

Joanna: "No problem, so what questions do you two want to ask exactly?"

Megan clears her throat, guess she wanted to ask the questions. I nodded and leaned back on the sofa.

Megan: "We just want to know what happened about two days ago, a late night on the eighteenth. We know you were there when it happened, so that's why we came here."

Joanna simply chuckles.

Joanna: "Well, you guys know what you're doing it seems, the eighteenth was a.. wild night to say the least."

Me: *"Yeah, we know. Can you remember any details from the party you all had?"*

Megan simply hit me on the chest, I nodded and backed away.

Megan: *"If you know anything, please, tell us. We're going to need all we can get."*

Joanna nods and takes a heavy breath, she closes her eyes and tells us everything she remembers.

Joanna: *"Right, there were four of us. Me, Victoria, Maxine, and Tricky. We got bored, so we invited a boy over, his name was Michael."*

Megan: *"I'm sorry to interrupt, but Michael who?"*

Joanna waves it off, basically saying it was fine.

Joanna: *"His name was Michael Fransier, we had invited him over to see which one of us he'd like to go spend a night with. He wasn't really too much of a confident guy. We felt bad for him, that's why we invited him over."*

We both look at each other, Michael was that kid I had befriended not too long ago. About a day ago. We look at her to see what happened next.

Joanna: *"Right, since he thought Maxine was so nice, he chose her. After they left, we may have cracked a few jokes. I never meant for it to be like this though-"*

I could see a visible tear come down from Joanna's eye, she was quick to wipe it though. It made me feel horrible, I suddenly wanted to cry too, but I held it in. I didn't even want to ask what happened next, because the answer was quite obvious. Her breaking down like that made it pretty easy to predict what went down after that.

Me: *"I can't believe I befriended him, I thought we were cool, but then he goes and ABDUCTS my best friend!"*

Megan sighs, she nods towards Joanna and pats me. Signaling it was time to go, I didn't say another word as we walked out, I was honestly speechless. I just grabbed my hat and placed it back on my head, we were going to visit Michael soon enough.

We both got back into the red station wagon and drove off towards Trevor's house. I refused to speak, I was still boiling from learning about my "friend" Michael.

Megan: *"I know it's tough being betrayed by one of the people you considered a friend. Trust me, I know. I'm sorry that you had to learn that about him. We're going to teach him a lesson once we get there though, aren't we?"*

I smiled and nodded.

Me: *"Yeah, we are."*

Megan: *"That's the spirit!"*

A few minutes later, we arrived at Trevor's house, only to see that the lights were out. He was asleep, of course. Well, tomorrow would work fine I suppose.

Megan dropped me off at home, we said goodbye to each other before she drove off. I nodded before going inside
my house.

Me: *"They won't like it but, I want to visit my parents."*

I take off my detective disguise and put on a black jacket with khaki pants. That was a good outfit, right? I nod as I start to brush my hair. I hadn't seen them in quite the while, I missed them.

I got out of my house and started walking over there, it'd be a while but I'd be able to make it.

Meanwhile, over at Trevor's...

Trevor appeared to be on the phone with someone. Someone unknown, he was pacing back and forth in his room and seemed to be in a heated discussion with someone.

Trevor: *"Yes, I sent them over. Don't worry, they'll be with him soon."*

The unknown person seemed to be heated, like they had had enough with Trevor.

Trevor: *"Don't worry, I know it'll work. They will do it, if not, I'll deal with them."*

Trevor then hangs up the phone and takes a heavy breath.

Back to Colson..

While I was walking over to their house, I started to hear noises from all around me. I slowly started to get suspicious. Something wasn't right.

As I had suspected, people were here. I wasn't sure who they were, but one of them I could make out pretty easily, Tye Andrews. He was back for more, before I could attack though. I was thrown onto the hard concrete by one of the others, I couldn't get a good look at them since it was so dark out here. I grunted as one of them pinned me down and socked me square in the face.

__Tye:__ "You thought you could embarrass me like that and get away with it? Think again."

Next thing I know, my head was rammed into the hard ground, I had been knocked unconscious. The last thing I saw was Tye pulling out a knife. Was he really going to?

__Me:__ "You... wouldn't, I know you aren't that stupid, Tye.."

I barely managed to form that sentence, I wasn't able to move. I had lost consciousness. There I was, laying on the sidewalk.

Chapter Seven: Stalemate

I woke up in a hospital, I suppose the only reason I had lived is because someone had come across me laid unconscious on the sidewalk. Shoot, can't believe I let them get the better of me. I couldn't move my head, it hurt too much.

As I slowly regained consciousness, I could see my parents sitting beside me. They had shown up? I just laid back and stared at them for a while before attempting to say something.

Me: "Hey, what's going on?"

I barely even heard myself, the bells ringing in my head were too much. Eventually, they stopped, and I could hear my parents.

Greg: "Son, do you know who was behind this?"

Jane: "Please, let us know if you remember anything."

I groaned and shook my head, I literally couldn't remember anything from whatever time they had knocked me out. I took a heavy breath. Soon as I did that, Trevor had walked into the room.

Me: "I'll be fine, I just need to go now.."

Trevor stopped me from getting up and forced me back onto the bed. I shooed him away. He'd then sigh and nod towards my parents.

Trevor: "Don't worry, I'm a friend of his."

Jane: "A friend? Well I suppose that makes sense, considering that you showed up.."

Greg: "Jane, do you really think we can trust him? Especially with our son?"

Trevor: "Mr. and Mrs. Matthews, I assure you that you have nothing to worry about. Please let me speak with your son for a moment."

He placed a hand on my shoulder. I simply swiped it away. I didn't want anything to do with Trevor right now. I didn't want anything to do with anyone right now.

Me: "How about you all just... leave? Get out of here."

Greg: "Son, we can't-"

Me: "GO!"

Greg pats Jane on the back and they both leave, Trevor however, decides to take a seat instead of leaving. I just stare at him.

Me: "Why are you still here?"

Trevor: "Come on kid, don't be like that. We need to talk anyw-"

Me: "Where is she?"

Trevor would lift an eyebrow.

Trevor: "Who? Where is who?"

Me: "Megan, she's the only one I need to talk to."

Trevor: "Kid, I can tell her once we're done-"

Me: "DO IT!"

Trevor: "Listen kid, you know better than to order me around-"

Me: "Do you think I give two craps? I need to talk to her, not you."

He simply chuckled.

Trevor: "Alright, fine, calm down. I'll call your girlfriend."

I just about socked this man in the face, but one of the doctors came in at that exact moment.

Male Doctor: "What exactly are you doing to Mr. Matthews, sir? Please leave him be, he needs rest."

Trevor: "Right, I was just about to leave actually. My bad."

Trevor would back away from me and exit the room, not without giving me one last look though. It was a look that said: "Watch your back" before switching to a jolly smile. I simply didn't pay him any attention.

The male doctor would come over to my bed with a cup of water.

Male Doctor: "Is there anything else you'd like sir-"

I nod and drink some of the water before tossing it on the floor. The doctor would back away.

Me: *"What I'd like is for you to get me out of this frickin' hospital."*

The doctor would simply walk outside to report what had happened I guess. Once he had done that, I got up and started to walk out of there, it was hard though. I was struggling to walk, but it seemed like it was going to be alright.

I got out of the room and started walking towards the exit, but the person at the counter had seen me and called the nurses. I had almost fallen over but one of the nurses had caught me, fortunately. I took a heavy breath.

Meanwhile over at Trevor's...

Trevor: *"Yeah, little punk is at the hospital as we speak. That'll definitely put the case on hold, sorry Megan."*

Megan: *"I need to go see him, you know which hospital?"*

Trevor: *"Yeah uh, the Saint Merades Hospital. The little man kept telling me to let you know he was there."*

Megan: *"Alright, thank you Trevor. Talk to you soon?"*

He simply laughs.

Trevor: *"Yeah, sure. Go ahead and see your boyfriend, give him a high-five for me."*

Megan: *"Whoa, he is far from my boy-"*

Trevor hung up, he seemed to love teasing the two of them. Not long after he had got done talking with Megan, someone else called.

Trevor: *"Oh, it's him again."*

He picks up the phone and gets up from his chair.

Trevor: *"Yeah, what's up?"*

Man: *"I assume that the boy is dead?"*

Trevor: *"Well, not dead. He's in the hospital."*

Man: *"What?? Hospital? You mean to tell me they didn't kill him?"*

Trevor: *"Hey, it's not my fault that those kids were scaredy-cats. I'll make sure to take care of them, boss."*

Man: *"No, Trevor. I'll deal with them myself, you just make sure that kid doesn't interfere with anything! Do you understand?"*

Trevor: *"Of course I do, you have a thing for yelling don't you old man?"*

Man: *"Just don't let me down, got it??"*

Trevor: *"Yeah, of course."*

Trevor hangs up and places the phone back in his pocket. He sits on his bed and sighs.

Back to Colson...

A few hours later and I'm at home, I still needed my rest though. I didn't want to rest, I wanted to find my friend. I needed to find my friend. I get up and go over to my room, I had been sitting on my couch the entire time. Before I had got to my room however, I heard a knock on the door.

Me: *"Who could that be? Why so late?"*

I walked over towards my door and opened it slightly, it was Megan. She seemed like she wanted to talk about something. I sighed and let her in.

Megan: *"You weren't at the hospital, they told me they sent you home."*

I take a deep breath and nod.

Me: *"Yeah? What about it?"*

She looks me dead in the eye before approaching me, stopping when she was a few feet away.

Megan: *"You were being stupid, Colson. What were you thinking? Walking out there on your own, you could have injured yourself!"*

Me: *"I needed to get back on the case, Megan. I needed to be out of there."*

She laughs my statement off.

Megan: *"No, you know what you really needed? You needed rest, you needed to stay."*

I shake my head slightly.

Me: *"No, I really didn't, Megan. I needed to get back to finding my friend-"*

Megan: *"Listen, I know you care about her and all, but you need to care about yourself too, Colson! Listen to me before you end up dead-"*

Me: *"I won't end up dead! I am not going to be in danger, I am going to* **be the danger.** *Do you understand me?? When those people see me they are going to be BEGGING for their lives! You hear me Megan Pryler?"*

Megan: *"Oh my god, I literally can't with you.."*

She brushes past me and walks off towards the door, preparing to leave.

Me: *"Do you understand now, Megan?? Don't EVER worry about me, if anything you should worry about those scum who TOOK Maxine from me!"*

That was the last thing she heard before she walked out and slammed the door behind her. I walk over to the couch and grab the remote, I turn on the TV and start to watch a documentary, but my anger at the time was boiling. I toss the remote onto the ground out of pure rage before leaning back in my chair.

Chapter Eight: Michael

January 21th, 2015

I woke up at around five in the morning, I figured that I could take a minute to sit down. I picked up the remote I had thrown on the floor yesterday and turned on the television.

The television currently displayed some sort of cartoon, but I was too old for that. I turned it back onto the news, apparently the police were still searching for Maxine, whoever had kidnapped her was good at covering up their tracks. I then saw something that shocked me. It said:

"Four males were taken from their homes earlier this morning, at three-forty five PM, no one knows of their whereabouts."

Missing person(s): Tye Andrews, Freddie Millsap, Wilson Hamilton, and Jerry Jermyn.

So now they're missing too? What is going on with this town today?

All of the others looked dark-skinned, aside from Freddie, who looked as if he was Caucasian, obviously we know Tye wasn't dark-skinned either. I sat back on my sofa before turning the TV off and sighing, those guys were jerks sure, but they didn't deserve this.

A few minutes later, I'm getting ready for school. It was almost time, I went to school as usual and had a pretty decent day there, actually. Although Michael was there, every time I saw him... my blood started to boil. I wanted to snap on him so bad, but that was for later. I'd visit him, on my own.

After school, after I had arrived home, it was time to go. Wait, no, not yet. His parents would be awake still, I needed to wait. I go to my room and put on my detective disguise. Black trench coat with a black and brown Homburg hat.

I sat on my bed and started to wait, it would be a while before I could visit that.. son of a.. alright, I need to calm down. I take several breaths before deciding to take a quick nap. I lay down and fall asleep.

After what I assumed to be a few hours of sleep, I wake up and instantly get out of bed. I decide now would be the time to call up Megan, although we weren't really on good terms from yesterday. I was being a jerk, I admit it. After waiting for about a minute, she answers the phone. I could tell she was irritated.

Megan: *"What? What do you want, Colson?"*

I took another breath as I prepared to speak.

Me: *"Listen, I know we aren't exactly on the best terms because of yesterday, but I really need your help-"*

Megan: *"No, what you really need is rest, now please Colson. Get some and stop torturing yourself."*

Me: *"Megan, this is important- I may have a lead on Michael-"*

She scoffs, I just knew she was shaking her head. There was no way she wasn't.

Megan: *"No, Colson, rest for a bit longer and then we can get this thing going. For now, goodbye."*

Before I said anything, she had hung up the phone. I cursed out loud and threw the phone onto the ground. I needed to go over to my parents house, they had two cars, maybe they could let me borrow one.

Skip ten minutes of walking and I'm knocking on my parents door. After a few knocks, my mother answered, clearly tired. It was eleven at night why wouldn't she be?

Jane: *"Who are you? Are you one of those detectives because if so-"*

I take off my Homburg hat and reveal my curly, light brown hair. My mother simply chortled.

Jane: *"What are you doing in that outfit Colson? Take it off!"*

Me: *"Wait, mom no. Don't, it's uhh.. cold out here."*

Jane: *"Right, what do you want?"*

Me: *"I kind of need to borrow a car..."*

She glares at me as if she was confused. I could tell her face said "You haven't bought your own?" She sighs.

Jane: *"Just take the car, Colson. Please, get out of here."*

I nodded, although Mom was a jerk she came through sometimes. Now what? I need to get back home is what, then I can take it from there.

I got home relatively quickly with the car, after I got in the house I took off my trench coat and got to work, it was time to find Michael. I get onto my laptop and go on the default browser.

Me: *"If I want to find him, I'm going to have to go deep.."*

I clicked on a white list website, that sounded like it may work. Problem was, I needed to pay. Of course, now what? I slammed my fist against the desk before starting to think.

Me: *"No, I don't need to pay, screw that."*

Somehow I needed to trick the website into thinking I had paid the money, but how would I do that? Trevor would be useful right now, but he'd probably be against me doing this as well. Wait.

Me: *"Maybe he's in my neighborhood somewhere, it's slim but possible.."*

I nodded and grabbed my trench coat, quickly rushing outside and getting into the car. It was about eleven fifteen at night, so maybe he was still awake, definitely. If there's anything I know about him it's that he's a night owl. I turn on my headlights and start to drive around the entire neighborhood.

Me: *"Come on, he has to be somewhere.."*

Skip another thirty minutes knocking on doors and saying the same thing over and over again: "Hey, have you seen Michael Fransier by any chance?"

My anger had boiled up the more I reached this tenth house. I instantly knew it was him, it had to be, otherwise I wouldn't be feeling such intense rage. I marched up to the door and knocked five times, no answer. Did it another five times, guess who opens it.. Michael.

I instantly calm myself down and try my best to maintain that tone, I looked at Michael and smiled politely.

Me: "Hey, would you mind if I talked to you? It's just I think you may know something about Maxine Taylor? Don't worry, it's just a couple of questions you know?"

Michael: "Of- of course sir, come right in, I don't mind."

I nodded politely towards Michael and sat down on the sofa. I waited for him to sit down before I started my questions.

Me: "First off, are you and Maxine friends?"

Michael: "Um, yes sir, we became friends not too long ago."

Me: "Alright, do you recall anything that happened that night?"

Michael: "Yes sir, I do. Um, so after me and her got home we talked a bit and we started to bond and everything you know-"

I couldn't hold it in anymore, the whole calm detective bullcrap. I told him to stop before shaking my head. I started to chuckle just a bit before silence fell upon the entire room. I then asked him:

Me: "Where is she?"

He suddenly sat back on his chair as I got up and started walking towards him. I stopped and got on my knees, making direct eye contact with him.

Michael: "Where is who? I don't know what you're talking about I-"

Me: "Maxine, where are you hiding her?"

Michael said nothing, I only continued to ask questions.

Me: "In your basement? Somewhere upstairs? Some... underground bunker? Tell me, Michael."

Michael: "I- I don't know what you mean, who are you-"

I got closer, we were both face to face now. I only continued to say the same thing.

Me: "Tell me, Michael. Where are you keeping her?"

Michael: "Listen sir, I honestly don't know, please.. leave me alone-"

Me: "TELL ME ALREADY! Tell.. me!"

My fist would slam against his couch as I slowly began to sob. I fell onto the wooden floor and just started bawling. Not long after, Michael had joined me in doing so. All I heard from him was a bunch of "sorry's" and "I don't know". He missed her too, I know he did.

__Michael:__ "I'm sorry okay? I don't know! Honestly- some guy just broke in that night and told me not to say anything.. he just took her and told me to keep my mouth shut or he'd kill me... that's all I remember that night!"

I suddenly stopped crying and wiped my tears, another guy took her? Who was it? I got up from off of the floor and patted Michael on the back.

__Me:__ "I'm sorry, Michael. I thought you were behind it all... the way that girl said it, it sounded like it was all you.."

__Michael:__ "It's fine, if it helps I remember some details about the guy-"

At this point in time we were both still wiping away our tears, I nodded to let him know that he could continue speaking.

__Michael:__ "Alright, well.. he had like a.. scratchy sounding and deep voice. Like a really really deep voice, his hair was all greasy and pulled back, his eyes were jade green and he had a slim figure, he was skinny."

My fists would bawl up again, it was time to pay that traitor a visit. Trevor.. you'll have some explaining to do..

I thanked Michael and went out to my car, that snake.. should have known there was something wrong with him. As I drove to my house all I could think about was Trevor, and how I was going to absolutely decimate him when I see him.

I arrived at my house, took off my detective disguise, put on some casual clothes, and went to sleep. Tomorrow was going to be an... intense day to say the least.

Chapter Nine: Traitor

While I was walking home to get a good night's rest, I heard some weird noises coming from around me. Was it happening again? No, who was it this time?

Me: "Jeez, who is it now? I've been attacked like this before, I won't let it happen again-"

I was hit with something in the back before I finished, I fell onto the ground and passed out. Not again, who did it this time? Was it? Probably was, he was probably watching me this whole time.. bastard.

After what I assume to be about five to six hours, I'm blinded by the light of day as a bag was ripped off of my head. I started to look around frantically and scan my surroundings, it was some sort of chamber that had brick walls, chains everywhere, and a trap door. I assumed this was under someone's house, probably Trevor's. I was tied to a pole and started trying to move, no use. I heard a familiar voice talking to me, I look up, and I see that snake, Trevor.

Trevor: "Well, welcome to my little hideout. You comfy?"

I shook my head and laughed, he really kidnapped me. Next thing I knew, a gun was pointing to my head. My glare shifted towards him, the guy who had taken Maxine from me. He simply smiled.

Trevor: "Kid, I'm going to have to ask you to back off on your little friend. Otherwise, I think I may have to do something that you won't like."

He pressed the pistol harder against my head, was he really going to do this? Well, I had promised that I would stop at nothing to save her, but was this really how it ended? With him shooting me in the head?

Me: "I would rather die, go ahead, do it."

Trevor: *"I wouldn't pressure me if I were you, kid. Choose your next words **very** carefully."*

I wouldn't say anything for a bit, I felt the pistol press against my forehead even harder. I don't know what happened, but I suddenly took a look at Trevor's arm, it took a bit but I noticed the slightest bit of trembling from it. I smirked before moving towards Trevor's face and saying these three simple words:

Me: *"Do it, coward."*

Trevor knew I wasn't taking him seriously at that point, he seemed to get ticked for a second, but he just placed the gun away from my head and proceeded to shake his own.

Trevor: *"Fine kid, I don't actually want to kill you, you win."*

After he had finished his sentence, I did a slight head tilt before starting my own sentence.

Me: *"Then let me go, and we can talk about this whole thing."*

He took a moment to consider it before nodding and coming over to untie me, unfortunately for him, that was just a big lie for him to let me go. As soon as he had done that, I managed to tackle him to the ground before consecutively throwing punches at his face. He deserved so much for betraying me and my partner, and who knows what he did to Maxine??

Me: *"You bastard, what did you do to her? Huh?"*

Trevor: *"What do you mean?? You don't know what you're talking about-"*

I had enough from him, I pulled him up from off of the ground and threw him against the brick wall before attempting to land a kick towards his gut, like I said, not much of a fighter.

Instead though, he threw an elbow onto my leg, which caused me to feel a decent amount of pain before eventually being punched in the face, that threw me onto the ground. I managed to recover, but it was a little too late for recovering.

He managed to land another hit, this time he had hit me with an uppercut. I was getting pissed off so I grabbed him and threw Trevor onto the floor, I managed to land a kick to the face as well.

He grabbed my leg and I fell onto the hard floor. Trevor managed to land another punch, after we both got up, I retaliated with a knee to the gut which made him fall yet again.

After that though, I was exhausted. We couldn't fight any more. Me and Trevor both were breathing heavily. I barely managed to say something for a bit, but I finally managed to get something out.

Me: *"Alright, now tell me, where are you hiding her??"*

I wiped some of the blood off of my mouth, staring at Trevor with a look of disgust. I figured that the perv needed time to recover. He got onto his side before finally saying something.

Trevor: *"Listen, you can surprisingly throw down, but I honestly don't know-"*

Me: *"Don't you dare give me that crap!"*

I ran over and kicked Trevor hard enough in the ribs to make him spit out some blood, he put his hands up, I guess that meant to stop. It made me want to hit him even more though.

Trevor: *"Listen, I- I didn't do anything to this girl okay?? I was just told to take her from Michael's place and bring her to someone."*

I got even closer to Trevor and took his gun, I pointed it at him to send the message that I wasn't playing around here. I'd kill him if I needed to. He got up and backed away from me.

Trevor: *"Hey come on, I'm sorry but I simply can't tell you who- I don't even know them."*

Me: *"I'm done with your crap, Trevor. TELL ME!"*

I tightened my grip on the gun, ready to pull the trigger if it was necessary. Trevor just shakes his head, I wanted to send another punch his way, I still didn't believe him entirely.

Trevor: *"Hey kid come on, look, I'll tell you okay? Just please put the gun down."*

I only got closer to him with the gun still in hand, basically doing the thing he didn't want me to do.

Me: "The gun gets put down when I want to put it down, understand?"

I was so ready to shoot this perverted bum in the head, but then he said something that shocked me. Although it could be a lie, something just.. told me it was true.

Trevor: "Alright alright, kid listen, it's all my father. This whole thing, it all has to do with my nut job father. I'll tell you everything."

Me: "Your father? Why should I believe that you-"

All of a sudden, I'd start to lower my gun. It wasn't intentional, I just started- doing it. I don't know why. I guess that was my body's way of telling me that he was telling the truth.

Me: "Alright, talk, make it quick. You already made me late for school you frickin' jerk."

Trevor: "Alright, listen, so my dad was living normally. He was a normal man. This was until my mother had called him to be picked up from work. Then, it happened.."

Me: "What happened? Spill it!"

Trevor simply nods, he starts to talk.

Trevor: "This happened recently, my father is Jon Gutenberg. Yes, the guy the police have been trying to catch for about four days now. He was at home one day when he got a call from my mother, Zyla Gutenberg who had called, she sounded like she was panicking. Before he said anything though, the phone had hung up. About a day later, he got a call saying that he should see my mother in the hospital, something had happened to her. Whatever it was, it killed her. We only know that it was someone else who did it, I'm sure that person is behind bars now, but after losing my mother, my dad lost it. His sanity just went down the drain entirely, and this is how this whole thing started, he hates the human race because of what happened to my mother. So that is why he has killed so many people."

Me: "Why are you in this whole thing then? I'm aware that it's really hard to lose someone you love but to start killing people over it?"

Trevor: *"My father forced me into this, I had no choice, he would have killed me if I hadn't accepted, I never wanted to do this."*

I would sigh and put the gun in my pocket, I helped Trevor stand up and took a look at his wounds. He was messed up pretty bad, but then again, so was I. I backed away and chuckled.

Before I could finish though, I was struck by a jab from the left of me, which had struck my eye. I suppose that was his revenge for kicking him, I wanted to strike back, but that would be wasting time.

Me: *"Alright, if you're telling the truth, where can we find your father?"*

Trevor shakes his head and sighs, that alone told me that he didn't even know. I stay silent for a minute before throwing my hat on the floor, how were we going to do this now? Trevor didn't know where he was, what was going to happen now? Was this the end of it all?

Me: *"So what now? What are we supposed to do? You don't even know where he is, how are we-"*

Trevor: *"I DON'T KNOW HOW OKAY? It has to happen though, it has to.. we need to stop this evil prick."*

Me: *"Woah woah, what do you mean "we"?*

Trevor places a hand on my shoulder, I was about to shoo it away but I felt like he was being sincere about all of this. I calmed myself down.

Trevor: *"I want to help you take him down, he's a monster that needs to be dealt with, as soon as possible. I need to assist you, believe it or not."*

I picked up my hat before staring at Trevor suspiciously, as much as we may have needed his help, he still helped kidnap Maxine. But, how were we going to do this without him? It takes a moment, but I shake my head before finally deciding that he would help us.

Me: *"Fine, you can help us. Just-"*

He nodded, all of a sudden I grabbed him and pushed him against a wall, I said with a venomous tone that if he dared betray us, we'd kill him on the spot.

Trevor: *"Got it, trust me, I don't plan on doing any of that. I hate the man that my father has become, as much as I don't want to, I need to take him down. This is my opportunity to do so."*

We both nod towards each other and get out of that chamber, wherever it was, it was far from where I was originally, I'll tell you that. Luckily, Trevor used his car to get me to my car before I went to my house, I nodded towards Trevor and he drove off. We'd continue this tomorrow.

Chapter Ten: Back-up

January 22nd, 2015

I wake up, go to school, all of that crap. We weren't here for that, we needed to start as soon as possible. As soon as I got out of school I called up Trevor and told him to come over, it was time to get busy.

Me: "Yeah, we're starting this today. Think you can make it?

Trevor: "Yeah, I'll be there soon, hold on. Let me get ready for this whole thing. It might take super long for us to find him."

I nodded and got into my detective clothing, I would put my gun in one of my pockets, I haven't had to use it yet. Something tells me when we meet his father, we're going to have to be very careful.

Something I didn't expect though, was Megan coming over today. As soon as I put my hat on to finish the outfit, I had to take it off along with the trench coat. What was I going to do about my bruises? I shrugged it off, I'd just tell her it was from Tye. I opened the door and just as I had expected, she saw my bruises.

Megan: "Colson, what happened to you? Where did all of this come from?"

Me: "Oh, this? This is just from Tye and his lackeys-"

She told me to stop speaking before she started inspecting them. She backs away and shakes her head.

Megan: "Looks like you've been out again, haven't you? Your wounds have only worsened Colson."

I sighed.

Me: "Listen, I just had to okay-"

Megan: "No no, it's fine, I'm just angry that you didn't tell me you were going."

I took a deep breath before I had finished processing what she had said, what? Was she going to help out now?

Megan: "Since you're so foolish, I suppose I have no choice. Let's go."

She brushed past me, I looked at Megan one last time before I decided to follow her.

Me: *"Listen, Trevor should be on his way shortly. After he gets here, that's when we start."*

She just sat down and gave me a cold stare for a few seconds before shaking her head. I could see why she was furious with me, but we really needed to finish this up soon. We don't know what exactly could have happened to Maxine at this point. I sigh before calmly placing my hand on her shoulder, Megan surprisingly didn't move and just stayed silent. I decided to keep my cool and tried to convince her to help me.

Me: *I know you're furious with me, but we really need to find her. I need your help, Megan. We don't know what could have happened to her by now, What if she's-"*

She told me to be quiet and nodded, I hope she understood what I meant, but suddenly she got up and started walking towards the kitchen, she stopped at the counter and took a heavy breath before her eyes shifted towards me.

Megan: *"Alright, when is he coming? It"ll be soon, right?"*

I then nodded, he was going to be here in about fifteen minutes. After that, we can start this whole thing, we were going to pay a visit to his father. He was going to pay, big time. We nodded towards each other before deciding to take our handguns with us. Something told me we were going to need them.

Megan: *"Wait, who exactly are we killing here, Colson?"*

It took me a moment to answer that question, I placed my hat on and took a heavy breath. Was this really necessary? Yes, it was. Who knows what he did to her? He could have done anything. Think about it. This guy was about to get what was coming for him this whole time, death.

Me: *"Jon Gutenburg, he's going down. Today or tomorrow, I'll take the life of Jon Gutenburg."*

Megan stopped me in my tracks, it seemed as if she couldn't believe what I was saying. I meant what I said, no take backs, at all. I was going to kill him. One way or another. I was getting revenge, no one was going to stop me.

Megan: *"Don't you realize who that person is? He is a **dangerous** person Colson. You won't come back alive, you realize this don't you?*

I stood there for a moment, nothing came out of my mouth. I didn't even move, didn't she know that I meant what I had said?

Me: *"As long as I'm the one who kills him, I could care less about what happens to me."*

All of a sudden, Megan's grip got tighter on me. She just spun me around to face her, I was confused at first, but that didn't last long. She raised her hand and slapped me. It actually hit pretty hard, causing me to stumble back a little bit. She wasn't kidding, she was strong enough to beat the crap out of someone if it was needed. Looks like I needed something to wake me up, though. After that slap I came to my senses. I sighed and regained my composure.

Or not, I didn't really say anything after receiving said slap, I just picked up my hat and walked out of the room, I needed time to myself. To be honest, I wasn't really thinking at that point in time. I sat on my couch and took my hat off, I placed it over my face and laid down, but I heard a knock on the door, he was here. I got up and opened the door, I let Trevor in.

Me: *"Time to start this thing, Megan is sitting in my room right now."*

Trevor: *"Right, we need to start now if we want to find your buddy."*

The urgency I heard in his voice, it worried me greatly. I placed a hand on his shoulder and stopped him.

Me: *"Why is that? Why do we need to hurry?"*

He sighs and gently removes my hand. Something was wrong, I just knew from how he said literally nothing.

Trevor: "Your friend may be in even more trouble than you think, kid. I would tell you more but I don't want to make this whole thing even worse for you."

I just nodded, we didn't really have time to talk. We needed to start, now. What were we going to do? The police are having a hard time finding him, how were we going to do this? I shook my head and just decided to sit down.

Me: "Hey, I need you all at this table, we can discuss this here."

They both sat down at the table, I couldn't believe that all of this had happened without even a week passing, all of this insanity, this whole thing.

Me: "Trevor, how are we going to do this exactly?"

Megan would nod, Trevor would have to know something for this to even work. Otherwise this was all for nothing, it would have been pointless. All of our work, all for nothing. There had to be something, right?

Megan: "Trevor, I'm sorry, I know it's stressful but we really need you to remember something for us."

Trevor wouldn't really say anything, We hated to put so much on him but this whole thing depended on what he remembered. Me and Megan would wait silently for an answer.

Trevor: "Give me a moment, I need some time to think. I may get something, just give me silence for a minute."

I nodded towards Megan, we both got up and patted Trevor on the back before going into the room. We knew it was hard for him too, having known that his father was a bad man and being forced to say nothing about it. He didn't want to do this. We both took heavy breaths before looking at each other. Megan got up first, and then I followed.

Megan: "Hey, if something happens to us, I just wanted to say something."

I hugged her, I don't know why, but I did. It felt like it was supposed to happen.

Me: "I know, don't worry. We'll be fine, I'm sure of it."

She shook her head, she then hugged me back, it genuinely was a nice moment. Something good to end on just in case, these were our last moments alive.

Megan: *"You don't know that for sure, do you?"*

I took a moment before answering, I shook my head and took a heavy breath.

Me: *"No, I really don't know. I want to take this time to say something."*

We stopped hugging, she then frowned. I hadn't been a good friend to her at all, if anything. I was a huge dunce to her. I take her hand.

Me: *"I'm sorry, I know I haven't been the best to you recently. I wanted to take some time to apologize to you, I was being so rude and I just wanted to let you know I never meant any of that."*

She smiles and nods, I let go of her hand and we hug one more time. We smiled towards each other before going back to Trevor. Who had hopefully thought of something by now. We sat down, he looked like he was ready to say something.

TREVOR: *"I may have remembered something, when I was taking some kids to him. I had to go to some kind of desert. It had taken what, about a few hours to drive there? It was the hottest desert I had been to by far."*

I got up and walked over to Trevor, there had to be something else that he could remember right? Right?

Me: *"Anything else? Please tell me there's something else."*

Trevor nods, and a whole minute of explaining later we're outside. If we were going to do this, we needed back up. Serious back up. We decided to try and convince some of the police department to help us out. We couldn't go with the three of us, Trevor had informed us that his father had men who were protecting him. Of course.

There was no time, but it was hard to convince them. After about two hours, they finally listened. We thanked them, and just like that, we had about twelve officers ready to back us up. Me, Trevor, and Megan got in the red station wagon, the officers got into three cars and we were off.

January 23rd, 2:00 AM

Who knew we would make it this far? Honestly, it was scary now that we were here. It was time to finally finish this, once and for all. All of a sudden, the weather started to get chaotic, it started pouring rain. There were flashes of lightning every few minutes or so, a major storm was brewing up. I could feel it, I figured that it was just one of those days, though. A storm is coming, so what? I leaned further into the seat, this was quite a bumpy ride. Trevor would start cursing, probably because of the weather.

Trevor: *"What is up with this storm? Where'd it even come from?"*

His windshields were getting pounded by rain drops, he'd have to use the windshield wipers every now and then. It was getting worse the farther we were going. The lightning started striking everywhere, mainly behind us, again, it was just one of those days right? I was starting to doubt going here, the weather was just being freaky right now.

Me: *"I don't know, but it's making me kind of freaked out. It just kind of started."*

He nods and continues driving, should we really be doing this? Was this the best idea? No, I needed to,I just didn't like sitting back and doing nothing. I wanted to help her.

I looked back, the thunder was still going strong, it was still striking behind all of the police cars, I took a deep breath and sat back, hat over my face. Megan would notice this and would try and calm me down. Was this really a good idea, audience? I don't even know anymore.

We were close, we had been driving around for about six hours now. Trevor was asking us if we were sure if we wanted to go here. Me and Megan would look at each other for a minute before nodding. We were ready for this.

Me: *"Yeah, we're ready. We'll do it."*

Trevor starts paying attention to the desert, he shakes his head before glancing at us again.

Trevor: *"You know, you can just let the authorities handle this, you don't need to go here."*

Me & Megan: *"We're ready to do this, Trevor."*

He nods and starts to pay attention to his driving again, we were ready. For sure. This was going to be tough, though, Trevor's father wouldn't be easy to take on.

Trevor: *"Listen, are you sure of this?"*

Me & Megan: *"Yes Trevor, we're ready to take on your father."*

Trevor: *"Well alright, you two have obviously made up your mind. I won't try and change it."*

We both nod, I could feel that we were close. All of a sudden, the storm just stopped. The lightning stopped, the rain stopped, just everything stopped. Trevor gave us a heads-up, we should be there soon. I take a look back at all of the cop cars behind us. I suppose we were all tense, because not another word was said for the remainder of the ride.

Chapter Eleven: Au Revoir

January 23rd, 8:00 AM

Trevor's car came to a stop. We were here, the police cars would stop as well, luckily for us, they didn't have the sirens on. So that wouldn't alert anyone, Trevor would lead the police to some sort of secret hatch, it was buried deep in the sand. He then came over to us.

Trevor: "Now, if you want to go in there and take them on, you're going to need to be very very careful. Got it? Don't get yourselves killed in there."

Me and Megan would nod towards Trevor before we all fist bumped each other. This was about to get very crazy, very fast.

After that, we were ready to go. We opened the hatch and jumped in, making sure to close it behind us. After all of this time, we were here, about to be in the most intense fight in our lives, and after we accomplished that, we could find Maxine. At last, I'd find my friend.

The police were ahead of us, they were exploring the area, taking looks left and right as they progressed down the secret hideout. The three of us nod towards each other before joining the authorities. This was frightening, but I had to do this. I couldn't leave her.

Me: "She has to be here somewhere, please tell me she's here."

Trevor pats me on the shoulder, he was trying to tell me that we were going to find her, that she was alright and that his father would go down.

Trevor: "You'll find her kid, I know you will, let's go."

I nodded, but before I could say anything, I heard gunshots come from in front of us. Was that them? Just in case, we decided to take cover. The shouts and yells of the police as they were unloading their bullets onto whoever was attacking them. Trevor signals for me and Megan to go.

Me: "Trevor, what are you doing? We need to help you–"

Trevor just shook his head and told us to go, I suppose he was going to help the police with the shootout, I took one last look at Trevor before patting Megan on the back, we needed to go.

As the sounds from the gun clash continued, me and Megan were trying to find our friend, we were rushing, so we bumped into a few tables here and there.

Me: *"Hey! Show us your face, you son of a bitch!"*

We would stop in front of some big, metal door, was this what we were looking for? Both of us gave a look towards each other before nodding, I walked up to the door. Before I could even touch the door though, it opened. As soon as I saw who came out of the door I recognized them, the ruler of them all, Jon Gutenberg.

We backed up and glared at the man, this was him, how did I know? The way he walked plus his clothes made it obvious. The three of us stood there for a while before one of us actually said anything.

Jon: *"Well, look who it is, Colson Matthews and Megan Pryler eh? Have to give you props, you made it this far."*

The psycho just walked straight past us, not saying another word. I gulped, but Megan gave me a look, we were going to follow him. Although we obviously had to do it silently.

Jon would go into the room where all of the commotion was, it was a.. terrific sight to see how the room was now, bodies were on the floor stacked on top of each other, blood on the walls, the whole police force was about gone. There was only one man left, this was a massacre.

I almost puked, seeing all of that blood, definitely something I wasn't used to seeing. I got myself together as we watched Jon, wondering what he would do next.

He simply gave his men a look, they fled almost immediately, to think an old man could be so.. terrifying. Was this really a good idea? I sigh and start to contemplate, what was there to contemplate? If anything, we were dead. Really dead.

That's when I felt a hand land on my shoulder, it was him. The man chuckled before looking at the both of us. I practically froze, was this it? This was such a dumb idea, why did I do this?

Jon: *:Well children, should we get started? I know exactly what you're here for."*

He shoved us forwards, guess we had no choice. We followed him upstairs, but then I realized something, where was Trevor? He sort of just vanished. Did Jon get to him without us noticing? I doubt it, Trevor's probably hiding somewhere, right?

So we walked up the stairs and this is when Jon went up to another door and slightly opened it, I could barely make out anything, but I knew the sicko had someone in there. Was it who I was looking for this entire time? If so, why would he reveal them to me? Why was he doing this?

Jon opened the door, that's when I saw her, she was alive. Max, that was her. A smile came across my face. Then I realized, bruises were all over her body. That's when I felt rage, greater than anything I've ever felt, I gave a look towards Jon.

Me: *"What did you do to her? Tell me!"*

He simply glared at me as a response, he walked over towards the horrified girl and started to untie her. He was letting her go? No way.

Jon: *"Don't worry about those, that's just from a few... sparring sessions we had."*

I let out a growl, as if this guy hadn't pissed me off enough. If you think I roughed up Trevor bad, you don't know how bad I'm going to beat Jon. He was already sick enough..

Jon: *"You want your friend so bad? Here, take her, I don't need her no more."*

Just like that, he released her, but as soon as he did, Jon pulled out a gun and shot her straight through the skull. My eyes widened as I watched my best friend collapse onto the rocky floor, she was dead. I froze in place before I noticed something, he was aiming the gun in our direction. It seemed like he was choosing who to kill next, me or Megan. I pulled myself together and got out my gun.

*   **Jon:** *"It's a shame really, to think you came this far, just to lose the one you were looking for."*

*   It looked like he was about to shoot me, but at the last second he switched to Megan and pulled the trigger, life felt like it was moving in slow motion, like a movie or something. I ran in front of her, taking the bullet for her, she was my friend, my best friend. I fell onto the ground as the bullet hit my chest and abdomen area.*

*   **Megan: "Damnit, hey Colson, you alright? Colson?"**

*   She yelled and pulled out her gun, last thing I saw before I passed out was them shooting each other at least three times. Damn, were we really all dead? Was this all for nothing? Those were my last thoughts before I passed out for good.*

Epilogue:

I woke up in a hospital bed, who brought me here? How am I still alive? I try getting up, but I just end up yelling in pain. The gunshot wounds, right. I lay down and sigh, it was all for nothing. I needed to see Megan, I wanted to know if she'd be okay.

"Excuse me, can I see Megan Pryler? I need to talk to her."

I couldn't really talk, but I managed to get the words out. The doctor shook his head, I stared at the bed I was in, was she already dead? I laid back on my bed and started to silently weep, as I knew what he would say next.

ONE MONTH LATER....

I would walk around the graveyard, flowers in my hands, it was for the both of them. I looked around at the gloomy area that was all around me. I had gotten them killed, it was all my fault. The wind was heavy and cold, the trees looked like they were on their last breath, everything around me was dead. I approached Maxine's grave first, bending downwards and placing the flowers right next to her gravestone. They were both dead, I was practically alone now. I then walked over to Megan's grave, placing the flowers right next to hers as well.

I shedded a tear before patting both of their stones, may they rest in peace. I looked at their graves one last time before making my way home, would Megan forgive me if she was still alive today? That is something I will never get to know, one thing I do know is that I'm never being a detective again, it was horrible. That time as a detective was awful, and the only thing that made it better and was there for me about the entire time was Megan.

Technically Trevor helped out too, huh, guess I'll go there and see how he's doing right now. I'm sorry, Megan and Maxine, I could have been so much better, and now you're both dead. I'm so damn sorry. I guess this was it, the end of it all. I would take one last tearful look towards the graveyard before I shook my head and walked off.